To Hazel and Daphne, it's enough just to grow. —M.S.

*To Michelle, the constant gardener and
mulberry tree of our family.* —G.Z.

Dial Books for Young Readers
An imprint of Penguin Random House LLC, New York

Text copyright © 2023 by Michelle Sumovich
Illustrations copyright © 2023 by Gracey Zhang

Visit us online at penguinrandomhouse.com

Library of Congress Cataloging-in-Publication Data is available.

Manufactured in China • ISBN 9780593112670 • 10 9 8 7 6 5 4 3 2 1
HH

Design by Lily Malcom • Text set in Stone Informal ITC Pro

The art was created traditionally using ink, watercolor, and gouache paints, on paper.

One More Jar of Jam

written by
Michelle Sumovich

illustrated by
Gracey Zhang

Dial Books for Young Readers

If you ever have a mulberry tree, you'll learn
there's nowhere sweeter to sit
than on branches, heavy with warm berries,

and draped with sparkling baubles and beads
to warn the birds, "No. This fruit is for me."
But they always snatch a few,
just a few,
every now and then.

You'll gather, wash, and smoosh
while your dad boils jars in a tall, silver pot,
sweating and happy as the kitchen fills with steam.

If you ever have a mulberry tree, you'll count
21 . . . 22 . . . 23 jars.
"How many are missing?"
Gone to sticky Grandma's table.
Gone to sweeten neighbors' bread.
And you'll suppose that you can share
just a few.
Only a few.

If you ever have a mulberry tree, you'll climb
bending branches
and shake with all your might

Until swollen fruit falls corner to corner
On an old sheet, freckled with berry juice.

If you ever have a mulberry tree, you'll lie awake
as wicked winds rage through your town,
and the constant thunder rumbles so loud and close,
you can barely hear the far-off coyote howl.
And you'll wonder if the berries will hang on
for one more jar of jam.

If you ever have a mulberry tree, you'll cry
when *thunk*—

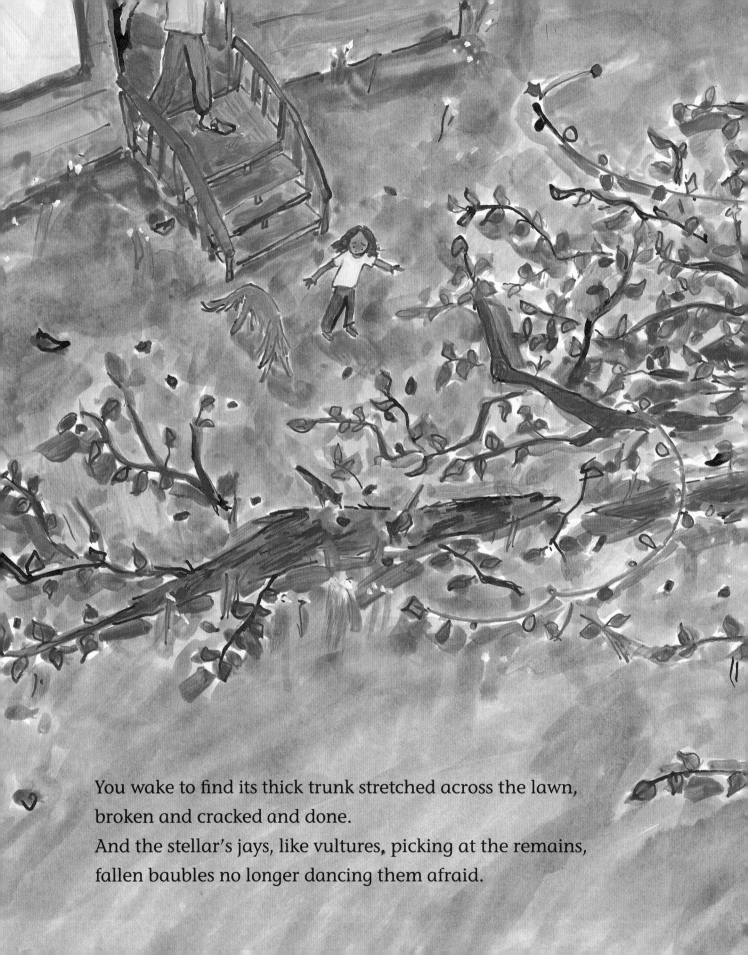

You wake to find its thick trunk stretched across the lawn,
broken and cracked and done.
And the stellar's jays, like vultures, picking at the remains,
fallen baubles no longer dancing them afraid.

If you ever have a mulberry tree, you'll slump
when it's a stump
because the summer is fruitless and dry as toast.

The fall's too stale, and the birds won't stay for bread crumbs.
The winter's too deep, and Grandma can't sweeten your day.
But when the snow melts, you'll see an old friend
and you'll want to say hello.

If you ever have a mulberry tree, you'll gather those who miss it most,

And celebrate things
that can no longer celebrate themselves.

You'll bring flowers and a little cake.
You'll count the rings,
Happy birthday . . . happy birthday . . . happy birthday . . .
And you'll mark the spot where *you* were born,
just seven wiggly lines away from the edge.

If you ever have a mulberry tree, you might
love it now more than ever.
Now that you know
it's enough
just to grow.

If you ever have a mulberry tree, you'll gasp
when suddenly silent, shiny leaves burst—
From stems
to shoots
to branches.

Happy birthday . . .

happy birthday . . .

happy birthday . . .

And you'll run to tell your family!
And you'll promise all your neighbors!
And you'll dance and shout and wait,

for one more jar of jam.